This Sunbear Book belongs to:

_____

ISBN 981-04-9885-3

Published by:
SUNBEAR PUBLISHING PTE. LTD.

First published 2003
Second edition 2004
Third edition 2005

Printed in Singapore

SASHA
visits the
BOTANIC GARDENS

Illustrated by Alpana
Written by Shamini

Book One: Sasha in Singapore

Sasha is looking forward to her visit to the Botanic Gardens.

What will she see there?

Trees, flowers and beautiful birds!

Sasha hears a tapping sound.

What's making that sound?

It's a woodpecker!

Can you see it?

Sasha looks out across the gardens.

There are tall trees and leafy plants.

"What's that over there, Mamma?"

"It's a shelter, Sasha. We can go there if it rains.

But it's not going to rain. It's a bright, sunny day!"

Sasha walks down a path.

She meets a little girl wearing pink.

There are flowers on both sides of the path.

What colour are the flowers?

Yellow, red and orange!

Sasha peers into a pond.

There are water lilies on the surface.

"Are there any fish in the water, Mamma?"

Sasha leans forward to look more closely.

Mamma holds on to Sasha's dress.

"Don't worry, Sasha! Mamma won't let you fall in."

There is a yellow oriole sitting on a branch.

Can you see it?

Frangipani flowers are lying on the ground.

They have fallen off the trees.

Sasha bends down to pick one up.

It smells delightful!

A mynah bird is sitting on a branch and watching her.

Can you see it?

Mamma places a frangipani flower behind Sasha's ear.

Sasha is not sure whether she likes it or not.

It tickles!

Mamma thinks Sasha looks very pretty....

A bulbul is looking at Sasha.

Can you see it?

Sasha lies down on the grass under a tree.

She looks up.

This is what she sees! A pattern of branches and leaves.

Perhaps you can try this the next time
you visit the Botanic Gardens....

Mamma and Sasha are playing hide and seek in the orchid garden.

Mamma hides. Sasha looks for her.

"Where are you, Mamma?"

Sasha finds Mamma among the pink and purple orchids.

Sasha is getting tired now.

She points to the park bench.

"Mamma, I want to sit down over there!"

There is a bright blue kingfisher on the park bench.

Can you see it?

He must be tired too....

The gardens are getting busy. There are....

babies in prams,

people walking and

children with their dogs!

Can you see them all?

"It's time to go home now, Sasha.

We'll come back again next week!"

Other Sunbear 🐻 Books
available in this series: